Thank you very much for your support of CCI and The Lemonade Mara!

Patti tara

the remarkable maria

Romario, Age 9

STORY BY Patti McIntosh
ILLUSTRATED BY Tara Langlois

Featuring drawings by the children of SMART, Suriname Art

Maggie & Pierrot
A CHILDREN'S BOOK PUBLISHER

THE REMARKABLE MARIA

Copyright © 2005 by Patti McIntosh

Illustration copyright © 2005 by Tara Langlois

Drawings by the children of SMART, *Suriname Art* reproduced
with permission.

PUBLISHED BY

Maggie & Pierrot—A Children's Book Publisher
67-21 10405 Jasper Ave NW
Edmonton, AB   T5J 3S2

EDITORIAL GUIDANCE BY M. Shaun Murphy

PRINTED IN CANADA BY Speedfast Color Press Inc., Edmonton

First printing November 2005

ISBN: 0-9739332-0-8

National Library of Canada Cataloguing in Publication Data
on file with the publisher.

www.remarkable-maria.com

For the children who inspired the story,
and the children who inspired the art.

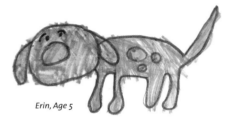

Erin, Age 5

"It is among young people that the heroes and heroines of our age are to be found. It is our job to furnish them with hope."

Kofi Annan
United Nations Secretary-General
15 January 2004
Keynote Address to International Women's Health Coalition

"Children can play with Maria."

Catherine, Age 7 1/2
Participant, ArtStart, Edmonton City Centre Church Corporation (E4C)
29 October 2005

Varun, Age 11

FOREWORD

The Remarkable Maria takes place in Paramaribo, Suriname; a predominately Dutch-speaking country in South America; 7448 kilometres from where we live in Edmonton, Canada.

Maria was inspired by events that happened in 2004 when Patti worked in Suriname with five AIDS Service Organizations (ASOs). There were problems integrating children from the orphanages into the schools. Some parents were afraid for their own children's health. But there was resolve on the part of the ASOs that these children not be isolated. This was where the idea for telling this story—its hopeful resolve—comes from.

We both travelled to Paramaribo in June 2005 to work with the children of SMART, Suriname Art, on the illustration of a story based on these events. With the help of translators and friends we started the workshops by talking to the children about HIV/AIDS, issues of discrimination and, over the course of the four evenings, read them Maria's story. We asked them to show us what Maria's experiences would have looked like.

We were thrilled by how seriously they took their art. We were also impressed by the level of compassion and understanding for the issues the children expressed in their drawings. You see their amazing drawings in this book.

We would encourage people to learn more about what is affecting Maria: HIV/AIDS, children's rights—and the arts. Much can be discovered by reading about the work of the United Nations Children's Fund (UNICEF) to empower girls the world over by promoting education, life skills and UNICEF's work on HIV/AIDS. UNICEF's *Convention of the Rights of the Child* is an amazing document. Articles 29 and 31 especially spoke to this project as they enshrine the rights of children to participate in the arts and culture and share their creativity with others.

There are the big and small fingerprints of many, many people who added to the creativity, and resolve, of this book—and we are very, very grateful to them.

Patti and Tara

P.S. A special thank you to the children of Edmonton City Centre Church Corporation's ArtStart program for also reading and drawing with us. And letting us see how you see *Maria*. Remarkable!

Ryan, Age 10

THIS BOOK BELONGS TO:

....

I have the same name as my mother, Maria, and I have been called remarkable. That makes me the remarkable Maria.

This is the story of how that came to be.

When I was little my father died.

My mother, my sister and I moved to my uncle's house. I got the feeling he didn't want us there.

He made us eat off separate dishes and stay in a different part of the house.

Soon, my mother got very sick. Then she had to stay in bed.

I cooked and took care of Wilhelmina. She's my little sister. Everyone calls her Willie.

Mrs. MacKenzie was my uncle's neighbour. Her dog had puppies.

When we were hanging our laundry, the puppies would sneak over and play with us.

My uncle wasn't very fond of Mrs. MacKenzie. She didn't care. She was always looking out for us. We knew Mrs. MacKenzie loved us.

When Willie needed glasses, Mrs. MacKenzie made sure Willie got glasses.

Every Tuesday night we would go to Mrs. MacKenzie's house and watch our favourite television show—Babbel Box.

We would sing and dance along with Babbel Box.

Mrs. MacKenzie usually sang and danced with us. One night, though, she sat at her desk and wrote a letter instead.

When I got home from Mrs. MacKenzie's, I would dance and sing for my mother and pretend to be on Babbel Box.

I would sing so loud, I think Mrs. MacKenzie could hear me next door!

Then my mother died. Just like my father. We had to move, again.

Mrs. MacKenzie helped us pack our few things. She told us good-bye and said, "You will always be my girls."

She gave us a radio and one of the puppies. We named him Pietr.

My uncle took Willie, Pietr and me to the orphanage and left us with Mrs. De Groot. She welcomed us!

We showed her our dishes. Mrs. De Groot told us, "You don't need separate dishes here."

She showed us our new bedroom. It was with all the other children's bedrooms. Mrs. De Groot gave Willie and me each our own bed—but we only needed one.

Willie and I were given just one chore at the orphanage ... folding laundry.

So, we had lots of time to play and dance ... and pretend we were going to school.

I was so excited about my first day of
school. We did each other's hair. I got
a new uniform and a new backpack.
I think Willie was jealous.

Mrs. De Groot took me to school on the first day. I met my teacher and some of the children. It was everything I had dreamed of!

One of the mothers recognized Mrs. De Groot and talked to her. I think they were arguing.

On the second day of school, my new friends told me they couldn't play with me. Their mothers had told them not to because I was sick. What did they mean I was sick?

I didn't understand.

On the weekend, we knew parents were saying mean things about us. We heard it on the radio. People said I shouldn't go to school with other children.

Mrs. De Groot found us listening to the radio and took it away.

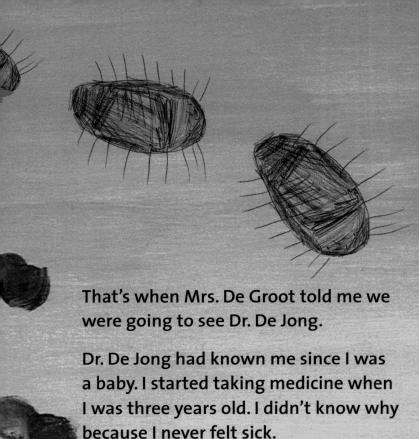

That's when Mrs. De Groot told me we were going to see Dr. De Jong.

Dr. De Jong had known me since I was a baby. I started taking medicine when I was three years old. I didn't know why because I never felt sick.

Dr. De Jong explained to me that my mother had a virus. This virus is like having bad bugs in your body. She told me a body can only cope with so many bad bugs.

My mother had more bad bugs than her body could cope with. That's why she was so sick.

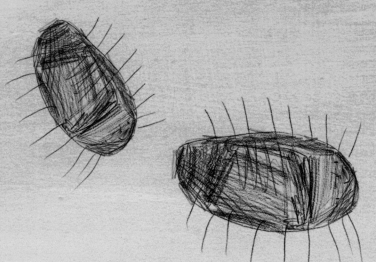

Dr. De Jong said I have some bad bugs in my body, too.

It is important for me to sleep well and eat good food.

If I take my medicine every day it should stop too many bad bugs from coming.

Willie doesn't have any of those bugs.
Not one!

Willie and other children can't catch
those kinds of bugs from me.

We can eat from the same dishes.
We can go to school and play together.
We can hold hands.

If I can hold Willie's hand, I can hold
anyone's hand.

Dr. De Jong told me.

Still, I was afraid. I did not want to go back to school.

Children will say mean things to me! They won't play with me!

I was so very worried.

I didn't want to play with anyone anyway. Or sing. Or dance.

I was hiding in bed when Mrs. MacKenzie came to tell me I was invited to go on Babbel Box.

I said, "No, I wasn't."

"Yes, Maria. I wrote a letter," she said. "They want you."

I said I didn't want to go.

She told me, "Maria, don't let people walk through your mind with their dirty feet."

I said I didn't know what she meant.

She said, "Maria, remember how much you loved to sing and dance for your mother. Don't listen to what other people say. You are meant to shine!"

I told her I didn't have a dress.

"Yes, you do," she said. And I did!

On Babbel Box, I was introduced as the remarkable Maria.

I was called remarkable for the first time. I was so happy!

But, I was nervous.

So, I took a deep breath.

I sang. I danced. I shined!

Everyone cheered! I was remarkable.

The next day I took my medicine.
I walked to school by myself.

Mrs. De Groot said that's what
remarkable girls do.

I knew I shouldn't worry but I wondered
if the other children had seen me on
television. What would they think?

When I walked into the classroom
some of the children smiled at me.
They had seen me.

The teacher asked me to tell the
class about Babbel Box. So, I did.

"Remarkable," said my teacher.
Then I sat at my desk.

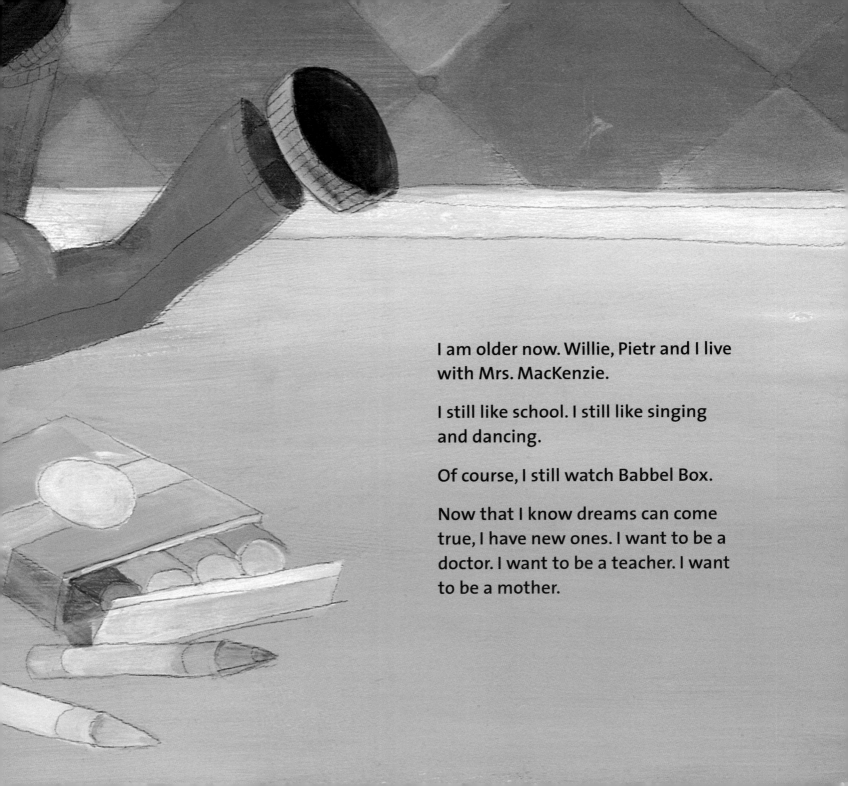

I am older now. Willie, Pietr and I live with Mrs. MacKenzie.

I still like school. I still like singing and dancing.

Of course, I still watch Babbel Box.

Now that I know dreams can come true, I have new ones. I want to be a doctor. I want to be a teacher. I want to be a mother.

the
Remarkable
maria for
president

I want to be president. The Remarkable
Maria ... for President.

SMART, SURINAME ART

Rochelle Abas, Age 9
Chester Ardjopawiro, Age 10
Roche Ardjopawiro, Age 9
Kamenie Bhagoe, Age 9 (Pg. 40, Maria's Drawing)
Marylin Blanca, Age 6
Gideon Dorff-Franklin, Age 15
Karan Ganga, Age 8 (Pg.19, Trees)
Varun Ganga, Age 11 (Pg. 14 and 21, Radio)
Kimberly Gesrooh, Age 8
Mitchell Ghafoerkhan, Age 9
Rayshree Goeldjar, Age 13
Dylan Halfhide, Age 10
Ryan Harripersad, Age 10
Lorenzo Helstone, Age 8
Lorraine Helstone, Age 13 (Pg. 16, Drawing on Wall)
Jallissa Janki, Age 8

Rhiannon Jjin-kon-koen, Age 10
Gero Kartowikromo, Age 5
Omar Kasyo, Age 16
Gillaume Mak, Age 6 (Pg. 17, Clothesline, Rainbow)
Carmelita Mak, Age 12
Safira Moore, Age 11
Barbera Oppenheimer, Age 12 (Pg. 8, Uncle's House)
Romana Ramdien, Age 6
Romario Ramdien, Age 6 (Pg. 17, Grass)
Kate Schuitemaker, Age 7
Vernon Simmons, Age 18
Jebienne Smith, Age 5 (Pgs. 22-24, Bugs)
Fariel Soeleiman, Age 10
Taisha Soekari, Age 7
Jair Vreugd, Age 7 (Pg. 16, Drawing on Wall)

Thank you!

Thank you very much to Hariette Helstone for her friendship and welcoming *Maria* to SMART.

Many thanks also to Lygia Blanca, Marten Colom and Maikel Koie A Sen for their great help and friendship.

Suriname Art
Beeldende vorming voor Kinderen en Jongeren (Visual art for everyone)

Ons erf
Prins Hendrik Straat #17A

Contact persoon:
Hariette Helstone, leerkradt beeldendvang
jhstone5@yahoo.com

Dylan, Age 10

Jallisa, Age 8

Kimberly, Age 8

Gideon, Age 15

Rayshree, Age 13

Roche, Age 9

Mitchell, Age 9

Marylin, Age 6

Omar, Age 16

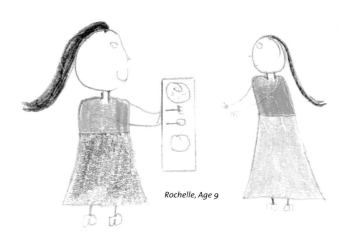

Rochelle, Age 9

Vernon, Age 18

Gero, Age 5

Carmelita, Age 12

Rhiannon, Age 10

Safira, Age 11

Taisha, Age 7

Chester, Age 10

Romana, Age 6

Lorenzo, Age 8

Kate, Age 7

Fariel, Age 11